We Need a Moose

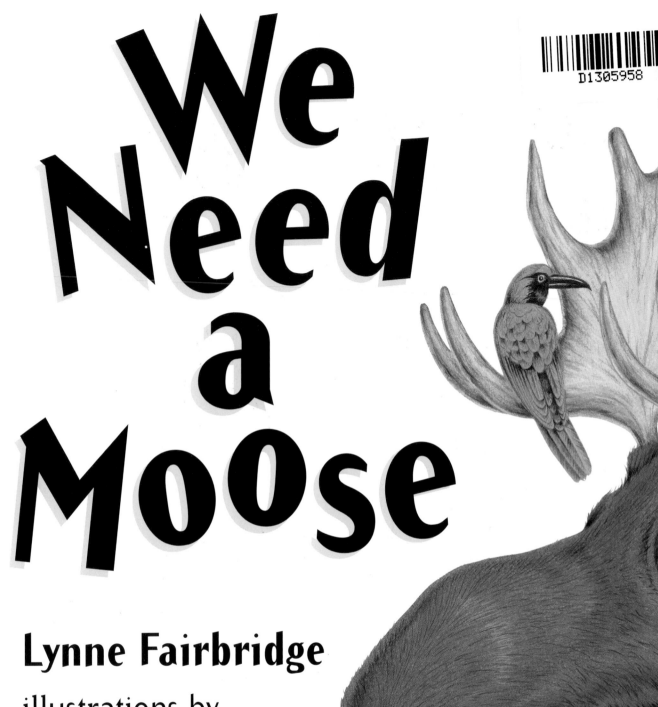

Lynne Fairbridge

illustrations by
Georgia Graham

 VICTOR BOOKS

A DIVISION OF SCRIPTURE PRESS PUBLICATIONS INC.
USA CANADA ENGLAND

D1305958

n Monday when I wanted to play, my mother said she had a hectic day.

"Come run with me, Mom. Let's race 'round the room."

"Not now," she said. "I'm busy."

So I bounced my ball on the backyard wall, and I thought of a funner room runner.

"**I** need a moose," I told my mother. "A moose can run, and we'd have fun. I'd ride around the yard on its back. Can I get a moose? I won't let it loose."

"We can't get a moose," my mother said as she ironed sheets for a baby bed. "They're too big for rides. And besides—imagine the size of a moose surprise on the rug!"

So when I went to bed, I asked God instead to send me a moose I could ride.

But He didn't.

On Tuesday my mother was cleaning again, so I went outside to play with my plane. But a wind blew up and my plane flew up on the roof.

"I can't get it down," Mom said. "It's too high."

So I stood and I stared at that plane on the roof, and I thought of a better plane getter.

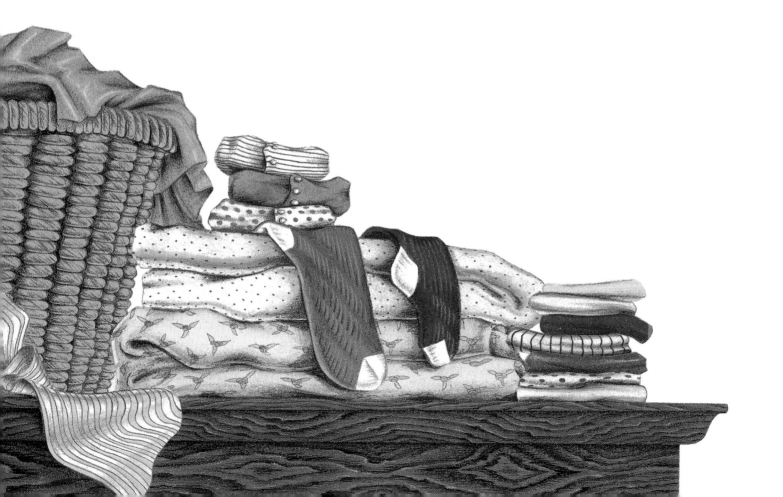

need a bird," I told my mother. "I want two. No, a few. Maybe five. Five friendly birds can fly very high and push that plane off the roof."

"We can't get a bird. That's quite absurd," my mother said, as she bent and kissed me on my head. "And besides, birds like to fly. They need the wide sky."

So when I went to bed, I asked God instead to send me some flying birds.

But He didn't.

Wednesday was wet and the wind was wild and I paddled in puddles on the street. But my mother was riled when I came inside with mud all over my feet.

"Please clean up," she said. "I'm tired."

So I took the mop and I washed and I sloshed, and I thought of a sweeter home greeter.

"We need a chimp," I told my mother. "A chimp will wait for me by the door and help me clean the mud off the floor. A chimp will be cheerful and not give me an earful for playing in the mud."

"We can't get a chimp," my mother said as she dried the rain from my head. "Chimps chew and they slobber and are quite a bother. And besides, I'll have quite enough to do caring for a baby and a boy like you."

So when I went to bed, I asked God instead to send me a cheerful chimp.

But He didn't.

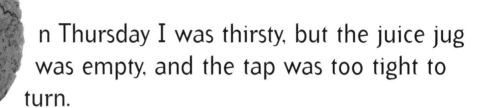

On Thursday I was thirsty, but the juice jug was empty, and the tap was too tight to turn.

"Try again," said my mother. "You'll learn."

So I went outside and I sat and cried, and I thought of a kinder juice finder.

"We need a camel," I told my mother. "A camel knows what it's like to be hot and terribly, terribly thirsty. He'd go straight to the sink to get me a drink; he might even keep juice in his hump."

"We can't get a camel," my mother said. "I'll get you juice before bed instead. Camels spit when they're mad and that would be bad. And besides, it's not hot enough here; they like warm desert air."

So when I went to bed, I asked God instead to send me a camel who likes cold.

But He didn't.

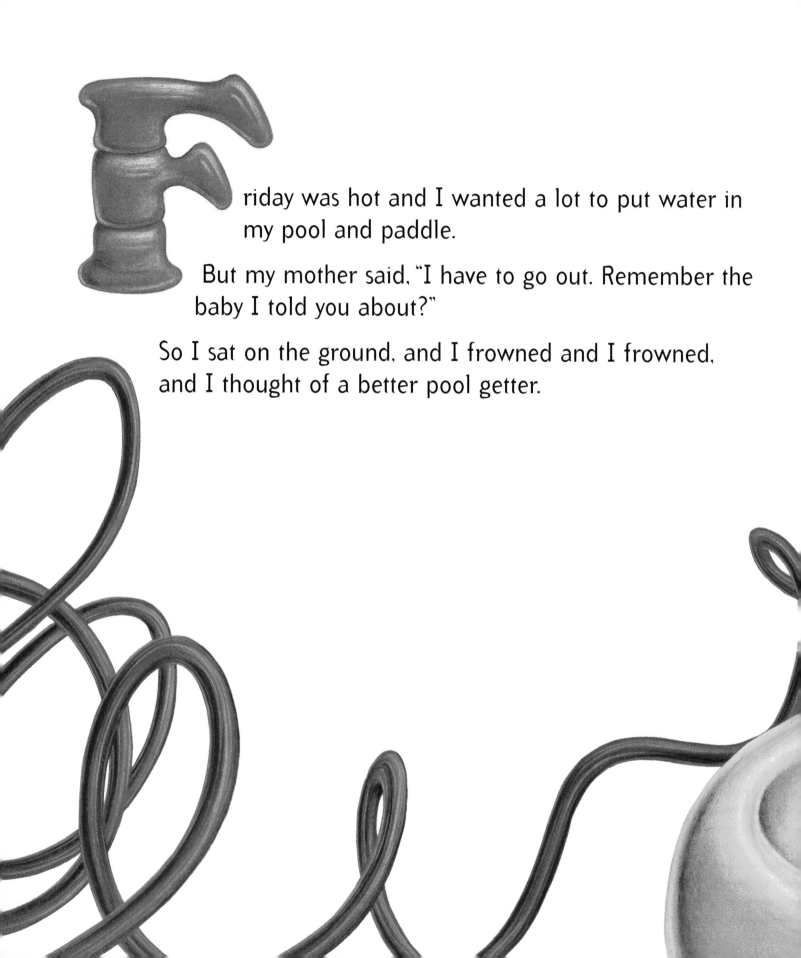

Friday was hot and I wanted a lot to put water in my pool and paddle.

But my mother said, "I have to go out. Remember the baby I told you about?"

So I sat on the ground, and I frowned and I frowned, and I thought of a better pool getter.

"We need a croc," I told my father. "Crocodiles smile, and when my mom sees that mile of sharp teeth, she'll fill up my pool."

"We can't get a croc!" My father was shocked. "They have claws on their feet and they eat too much meat. And besides, they often eat small boys for a treat."

When I went to bed, I asked God instead to send me a not-hungry croc.

But He didn't.

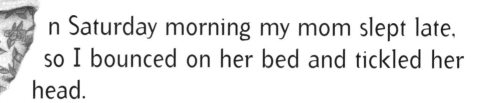

O n Saturday morning my mom slept late, so I bounced on her bed and tickled her head.

"Don't do that," Dad said. "She's exhausted."

I stood by her side and I stared and I tried to be quiet as a mouse as I waited.

Then she opened her eyes and gave me a smile.

"Guess what God sent to us in the night."

So I looked 'round the room to find my croc or a chimp or a bird of some kind.

"Look over here in this crib," said my mother. "God has sent you a brand new baby brother."

H e didn't have wings or hooves or claws, and he didn't have any teeth at all. But my mother said in a little while, he would smile, then sit, then crawl. And after that, when he was bigger, she figured we'd have a ball.

So Sunday was a fun day, and I thanked
God for this answer to my prayer—that
He sent a little brother who would love
and care.

And it didn't take much for me to see
that a brother was much better than a
chimpanzee.

Or even a moose.